Get Back
in the
BOOK!

Dedicated to educators in every capacity—
especially my most influential, Dad and Mom
——LARRY ISSA

To Nanny, for making it possible
——EMMA CHADWICK

ISBN 978-1-9999267-0-0
First published in 2019 by Kalamus
an imprint of Akkadia Press and LMI Design

Text: Larry Issa
Illustrations: Emma Chadwick
Editor: Claire Glasby
Design and typesetting: LMI Design

This book is typeset in Ysobel 16/22, Slate 8/11, and Charter

Printed and bound in Guangzhou, China
by Everbest Printing Investment Limited an
accredited ISO 19001 and FSC-certified printer

Special thanks to Emma Chadwick, Carl Gibeily, Claire Glasby,
Anne Renahan, Joe Jamaldinian, Nadia Habib, Jade Garrett,
Susan Serafin, Leslie Silvey, Gary Wells, Linda Wells,
Stephanie Trinidad, Lisa Huang and her production team,
Dad, Mom, Ramzi, Jackie, Dana, and Danny
——L. I.

Get Back in the Book!

Larry Issa
Emma Chadwick

Kalamus

Danny loves to write and draw.

He is writing a story about a
baker who bakes magical cakes...

Sticky fudge
Pudding.
with sweet
gingerbread.

FOR ARVIE THE acrobat when you stand on your head

"Finally finished!"

Carefully, Danny places the book in his backpack.
Tomorrow is show-and-tell at school.

He can't wait to show
everyone his book.

Danny dreams of the characters he has created.

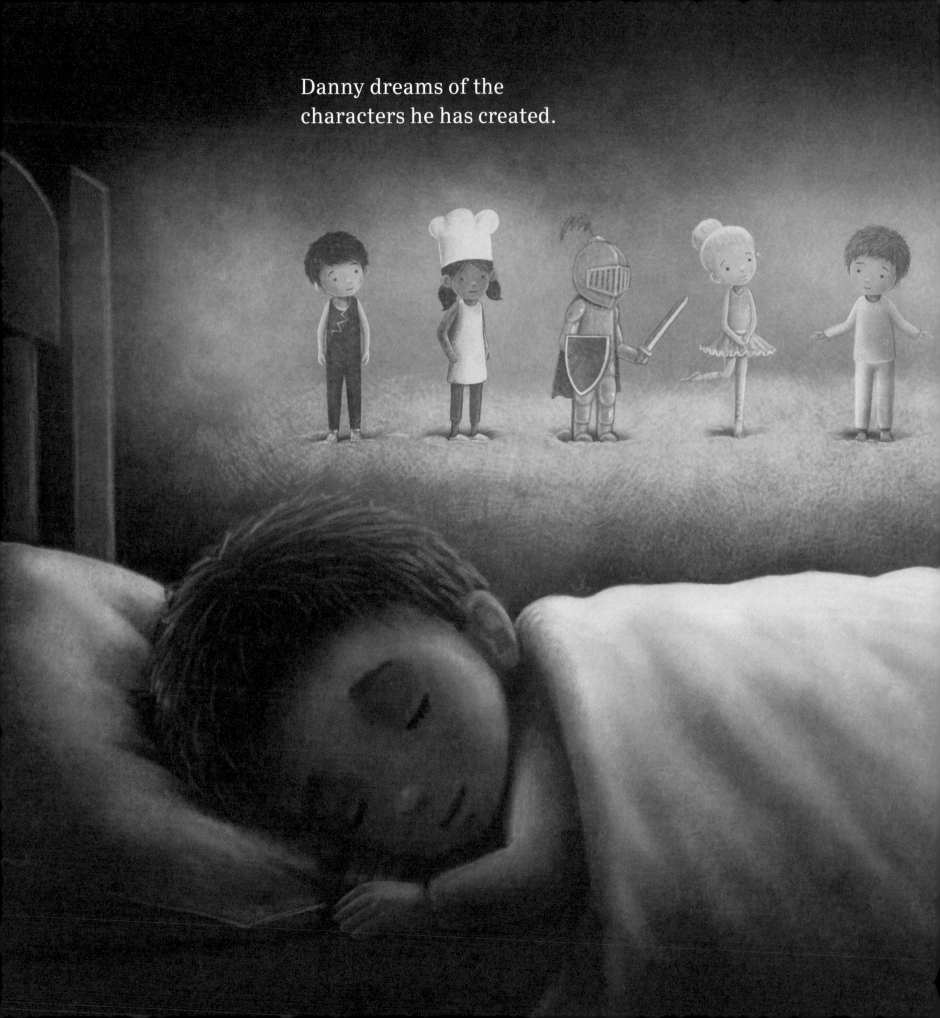

CRASH!

Danny wakes up with a fright.
What was that noise?

He reaches out
to turn on his
bedside light.

"Helloooo?
Is anyone there?"

His backpack has fallen on the floor.

"Quick, let's get out of here!"

"Ouch!"

"Open the zipper."

"Hurry up!"

Ziiiiiiiiiiiiiiiiiip

His backpack starts to open.
"Wh-wha-what's happening?"

Quick-as-a-flash, a tiny acrobat
leaps out of the bag and into the air.

"We're freeeeeeeeee!"

Danny grabs the acrobat as he flies past.

But wait, haven't we seen him before?

"I know you! You're Arnie the acrobat.
You are from my story!"

Danny pulls
out his book.
It looks different.

"My book!
Where have all
my drawings gone?"

He peeks inside his
backpack and can't
believe his eyes!

"Hello, Danny!"

One by one, they scramble out.

"What are you all doing out here?
Please get back in the book!"

"No we can't, Danny, we're too scared!
Ike the dinosaur is going to eat us!"

"But Ike doesn't eat any of you.
  Here, let me tell you how the story goes."
  Danny starts to read...

Light, fluffy
cupcakes for Belle
and the Ballerinas
after your twirls.

Brie bakes the
right cake for
right

The tiny characters listen in wonder to Danny's marvelous tale.

Danny finishes his story and looks at his new friends. "Now that you know Ike won't eat you, will you please get back in the book?"

"No thanks, Danny!"

"Who wants to be stuck in a book
when it's so much fun out here?"

"We want to see
amazing places
and different faces!"

"A good book **can** take you
to some amazing places..."

...to the Arctic...

...to Africa...

...to Arabia...

...and Australia!

"Just think about all the people
who will read about you."

"Are **you** reading about us?"

"So, what are
you all waiting for?
Get back in the book!"

"Let's go, we have a story to tell!"